DETECTING HALEY

A Walter Anchor Ghost Detective Story, Case #1

ROBERT J. MCCARTER

Little Hummingbird Publishing

Detecting Haley

A Walter Anchor Ghost Detective Story

Cover images by Benjamin Balazs from Pixabay

Version 1.0, May 2019

Version 1.1, January 2020

ISBN: 978-1-941153-10-9

Visit Robert's website at: www.RobertJMcCarter.com

Published by:

Little Hummingbird Publishing

P.O. Box 23518

Flagstaff, AZ 86002

www.LittleHummingbird.com

Little Hummingbird Publishing is a division of Arapas, Inc. Find more about Arapas at: www.Arapas.com.

✿ Created with Vellum

- **Case 1: Detecting Haley** (also part of *Life After: Stories of Life, Death, and the Places in Between*)
- **Case 2: The Ghost Bride's Gift**
- **Case 3: A Long Hard Fall** (coming March, 2020)
- **Case 4: Death of a Dentist** (coming May, 2020)
- **Case 5: A Hollywood Kind of a Murder** (coming July 2020)
- **Case 6: The Red Arrow Murders** (coming September, 2020)
- **Unfinished Business: The Cases of Walter Anchor Ghost Detective** (coming October, 2020)

Chapter One

I HATE BEING A GHOST. DON'T GET ME WRONG, I'M GLAD to have consciousness and all that, but it's the little things I miss. Like the taste of a tender, juicy steak and a cold beer. The sound of an audience clapping for me. The feel of a pair of dice in my hands. The rough texture of a cat's tongue. The searing heat of the Tucson sun.

But so what? I'm a ghost and I've got a murder to solve. *Mine.*

We ghosts usually have unfinished business, and since I haven't heard the "call," I figure my unfinished business is my murder—that's what's keeping me earthbound. The "call" is that glorious event when a ghost moves on to the next stage of their afterlife. Opinions on exactly what this is varies, but I'm ready to be out of here.

Not that I'm qualified to solve murders or anything. I was a dentist by trade and before that an out-of-work actor.

These thoughts rumbled through my mind as I stared at the dead body on the grimy carpet below me.

"Well?" Emily asked. She looked at me with her

ancient green eyes that inhabited her round baby face. She has short, curly blonde hair that reminds me of Shirley Temple when she was a kid. Emily died when she was four years old, but now she's eighty years dead. There is a lot of wisdom packed in that adorable little body. But I gotta tell you, it's more than a little disconcerting.

"What?" I shrugged, looking at the dead body and her ghost. She was in her late twenties with long brown hair. Her blood had pooled and congealed on the light-blue carpet. Her ghost was gape jawed and clearly in distress, the thin silver cord that attached her soul to her body still intact, going from belly button to belly button.

"You've got to do something," Emily insisted. She has an adorable lisp, so it was "You've got to do *thomething*." I won't write it that way so you don't go crazy reading my little story, but you get the idea.

"Why?" I asked.

"The poor thing is suffering," she said, pointing at the wispy mess of a ghost, its mouth open wide, a pitiful moan escaping from its throat.

"You do something," I said.

"I am. My plan is to whine until you do something." Emily may be eighty years dead, but there was still a lot of four-year-old left in her.

I sighed. "This is a distraction, Emily. We are here tracking a clue to my murder."

"Yeah, and that clue took us here. To her. I think we need to investigate."

I nodded, stooping down and looking at the body. "Maybe we can snoop around and get Banquo to come take care of the bardo-brain." The bardo is a place we ghosts often find ourselves when things don't go so well and this ghost had all the signs.

"Should I go get him?" Emily asked, her voice going all

high when she said "him." The girl has a great big crush on Banquo. He's kind of the ringleader of our graveyard community, and Emily has had a thing for him since he first came there around ten years ago. He is an expert, as much as anyone is, in helping these distressed ghosts.

I looked closer at the corpse, getting down low so I could clearly see her face. I felt a tingle of shock flow through my ghostly form. I knew this woman. She temped at my dental practice the month before I was murdered. And now she lay here also murdered.

Even though I wasn't experienced at the detective thing at the time, the knife sticking out of her back gave away the "murder" part of the equation.

My name is Walter Anchor. I solve murders. This is my first case.

Chapter Two

"Yeah," I said to Emily, "go get him." With a girlish squeal and a "pop" she was gone, and I was left there with the dead dental assistant.

I looked around the grubby little Tucson apartment. A small bedroom, a kitchen with dirty dishes everywhere, a cracked LCD TV in the living room. I then looked at the victim again. Tall, slender, dressed in designer jeans and a pastel blue blouse stained with her own blood. Her nails were well manicured and the makeup on her face expertly applied.

This was not her apartment.

Being a ghost detective is all about observation. It's not like you can question witnesses, or root through their garbage, or run a background check. What you can do is watch and observe, twenty-four hours a day, seven days a week.

The ghost groaned and I got up and looked at it. Her ghostly appearance was nothing like her physical appearance. She had a diffuse vapor-like form, her eyes wide, her limbs vague stubs. She was lost, trapped in her own personal hell, a place known as the bardo. This torturous state is not uncommon for us earthbound spirits, and even less uncommon for the murdered.

I have never been in that state. I have Emily to thank for that.

The ghost moaned again and I listened carefully. The one great advantage of being a ghost detective is that you can sometimes talk to the dead.

"Haley," I said, remembering her name. "It's me, Doctor Anchor. Can you tell me what happened?"

"Blaaa," she hissed, her eyes meeting mine briefly. "Blaaaack Shooooes."

"Black Shoes?" I asked.

"Blaaaack Shooooes," she moaned again. In fact, the need to listen carefully was overkill. Haley just kept saying it over and over again, the moan of it becoming a kind of eerie mantra as I went back to examining the body.

The knife was thin and long, buried to the hilt between two of the vertebrosternal ribs. It had pierced her heart, she hadn't been alive long; the person wielding the knife had known what they were doing.

I made a slow sweep of the apartment and found out several things. Someone named Roger Coptic lived there, he was a slob, a drug addict (the used needles in the trash can were a dead giveaway), and hadn't been home in quite some time (the wilted marijuana plants in the bathtub helped with that).

Which led to the question, what was a nice girl like her doing in a place like this? And, what did this Roger Coptic have to do with my own murder?

Chapter Three

MAYBE I SHOULD PAUSE AND GIVE YOU A LAY OF THE land. Like when I was alive and a patient would come in for a procedure. It seemed to always help for me to sit down with them and tell them what to expect, warn them of the difficult parts, and make sure they understood both the risks and the rewards. Especially the unpleasant procedures like a root canal or an extraction or root planing. Ah, hell, who am I kidding? I was a dentist, most of the "procedures" were unpleasant.

I would put on my deep actorly voice and tell them the toughest pieces in the calmest, most reassuring voice possible.

So here goes.

The world thinks I committed suicide, which I frankly find depressing. I know, suicide is pretty high in my line of work, but I was a happy dentist. Seriously, I was. I loved my job, I loved my staff, I loved my patients. My life wasn't perfect, I had been divorced for several years and found myself a bit phobic about relationships (could explain why my best friend as a ghost appears to be a four-year-old), I had a bit of a gambling problem (okay, okay, by a "bit," I meant "massive"), and I hadn't talked to any family members for a few years.

So yeah, there was the good in my life and the not so good. Just like any other human on the planet, you peel back the layers you're going to find some nasty stuff. Me, I was lonely. I worked too long because I didn't have much else to do, except for gambling. It's hard to feel alone when you're throwing the dice at the craps table and people are cheering you on.

Anyway, where was I? Oh yeah… lay of the land. So about six months before finding Haley murdered, I had been working late, finishing my charting, avoiding going back to my crappy apartment, when I was murdered. It wasn't anything spectacular, I had just sat down in one of the dental chairs and closed my eyes for a moment—I must have fallen asleep. Next thing I knew I was a ghost hovering over my own body.

It was a shock, to say the least. Looking at my body, a hypodermic still sticking out of my arm, a drop of blood at the injection site. It looked like a suicide, but I know it wasn't.

I spent several months in the dental office—and not by choice, I must say—watching. I guess you could say I was haunting the place. I didn't really "do" much of anything but creep people out occasionally, but I watched and waited and listened.

My partner in the practice, Doctor Wheeler, kept things going and soon people started talking about me. Specifically, talking about me like I wasn't there.

Let me give you a piece of advice. If you find yourself a ghost, get away from the people you knew if you can. This shouldn't come as a surprise, but folks don't see you the same way you see yourself. There are misunderstandings and your intent is not always apparent. The experience can be disturbing to say the least.

I could give you lots of examples, but let's just say that some of my employee's feelings about me were rather surprising, some liking me way more than I thought proper and others disliking me more than I thought possible. Which makes sense, no one sees you like you see yourself. It just isn't comfortable.

So, I was stuck in my dental office, and as the picture of the events of that day became clear, I decided I needed to find my own murderer. One clue at a time, one step at a time.

It's not like I had anything else to do.

Chapter Four

WHEN I HEARD TWO POPS, I LOOKED UP FROM HALEY'S body and saw Emily and Banquo. Emily was beaming and looking up at the big-bellied man. Banquo stepped forward, his eyes on me and then the ghost.

"Good evening, Walter," he said.

"Banquo," I replied. Look, I give the guy his props. He knows a lot and does a lot for our little community, but I just ain't in the fan club. Not one of his students.

Now it could be that he is also the leader of the Midnight Circle—the nightly gathering of the ghosts at the graveyard—and that irks me a bit. Sure the guy's an English Lit professor, knows a lot of Shakespeare and other plays by heart that he leads the circle in. But maybe they should give someone with acting experience a chance every now and then. Someone like—

"Have you tried to reach her?" he asked.

I snorted in response. I knew he knew the answer. He just wanted to hear me say I couldn't be bothered.

"I know you can help her," Emily said to Banquo, her little lispy voice higher than usual. She's one of the reasons

I don't feel the need to faun over Banquo—she does it more than enough for both of us.

"My boy," Banquo said to me, "you really should take the time to help those in need."

I straightened up and met Banquo's gaze. "I am," I said, pointing at myself with both my thumbs. "Who else is going to solve my murder?" I moved away into the bedroom to see what I could see there. I left Banquo, Haley's ghost, and Emily to do their thing.

ALL THAT TIME I spent haunting my dental practice I learned many things, but most of them not useful to solving my murder.

Mostly what I learned watching and listening was the messy reality of humanity: unhappiness, affairs, depression, petty bickering, addiction, and the like. I also saw the good stuff (kindness, love, and generosity), which I had known was there too. But, it was the quantity of the not so good stuff that surprised me.

Ultimately I did find a clue to my murder. There was something off about Midge, my office manager. It was the guilty look she kept getting on her round Midwestern face when no one was looking. She knew something.

When I could finally leave the dental office (that's a whole 'nother story), I started following her everywhere and eventually came the day when the letter arrived. It was a plain white envelope with her address shakily written in blue ink. She had rushed into the bathroom with it, avoiding her husband and daughter, and opened it.

It said, "If you need to reach me again about your

financial problems, drop a note at this address." It was followed by the address of the gross apartment Haley died in.

Midge's hands shook as she slowly tore up the letter and flushed it down the toilet. At first when I saw that guilt on her face I had been angry; seeing her scared like that softened that feeling. She knew something, but whatever she had done, she had been coerced.

I shook right next to Midge, my ghostly form turning diffuse, my vision tunneling in, a crushing depression descending on me.

Conspiracy… had there been a conspiracy to kill me? Was Midge part of it? It looked like my death was part of something larger. I was nobody, just a failed actor turned dentist. Who would want me dead?

I would have fallen into the bardo right then and there if it hadn't been for the little voice that said, "Not cool, let the lady go to the bathroom in private. What kind of sicko are you?"

I saw the little ghostly form of Emily, her hands on her hips, her mouth a sneer.

Seeing her shocked me back to myself. "Who are you?" I asked.

Chapter Five

As I looked around Roger Coptic's bedroom with its unmade bed, its piles of dirty laundry and unopened mail, I tried to tune out Emily and Banquo. Her voice was an octave higher than usual as she said things like, "Oh, I so know you can help her," or "Did anyone ever tell you you look like Lawrence Olivier from when he played King Lear at the West End in London?" or "What are you doing later tonight?"

Banquo's replies were curt but courteous. And then at some point things got quiet out there, which was fine by me.

"I had a thought," Banquo said to me, from the door of the bedroom.

I looked up from the grease-stained pile of mail, not answering, but giving him my best "can't you see I'm busy doing important things" look.

"I think you should try to pull her from the bardo. She might have some information for you about her murder and that might help you along."

Emily stood behind him and to his left, her eyes all

doey as she stared up at him. "Walter," she gasped. "Isn't that a brilliant idea? That was brilliant, Banquo."

And it was a good thought, but I certainly didn't want to say that in front of Emily. "I guess," I replied. "But, I have no idea how to—"

Banquo's face lit up like a kid on Christmas morning. "I'll be happy to show you what I know, my boy." Banquo loves to teach, it's really his thing. And while I appreciated the thought, I can't stand it when he calls me "my boy." I'm not his boy.

BANQUO IS CHUBBY, bald, sixtyish, and grey haired. He slowly paced around Haley as he lectured, his hands clasped behind his back. Very much the professor.

He started by explaining the bardo—I know what the bardo is. It's that place ghosts often get stuck where they are reliving the worst of their past, stuck in their regrets. It's hell, quite literally. Haley was there, no doubt. Her eyes were wide, her mouth slack, B-movie-ghost groans coming out of her mouth. And I felt for her, I did, but it's not like there's an easy foolproof five-step plan to get someone out of the bardo.

"The essence of it," Banquo said, "is finding something more important to her than her suffering."

"Oh," I said in my best dry sarcastic tone. "That's all."

Banquo stopped and looked at me. He has this penetrating gaze that, if the rumors around the graveyard are to be believed, can see directly into your soul.

"People like to suffer," I said by way of explanation, his eyes focusing on mine. I really didn't want him looking into my soul. That grunge and disorder that has its home there is mine, all mine. Emily looked at me too, her little brow furrowed. "Really, they do," I continued. "Look at anyone you knew when they were alive. How many ways did they make their life harder, how many things couldn't they let go of that would have made them happier? How much—" I cut myself off when I saw Emily's face, her lower lip was quivering and she looked like she was about to cry. I knelt down in front of her and said, "What is it, honey?"

As little girl tears rolled down her ghostly face, she said, "My mom, after I died. She couldn't let it go, she suffered so much. I..."

I carefully modulated my ghostly form (a must for a ghost to touch another ghost) and pulled Emily in for a hug and let her cry. She was in the past, and when she was like that she was much more the four-year-old girl and much less the eighty-year-old ghost. I caught Banquo giving me a "look what you've done now" look.

After she was done crying, she growled, "Get your mitts off me, you perv."

I didn't take it personally. It was Emily's way of telling me she was all right.

"Now," Banquo said, clearly about to resume his lecture, "you knew her, what might be more important to her than her suffering?"

"Knew her?" I said. "She temped for me for a month. We weren't exactly bosom buddies." I mean, yeah, there a little more to it than that, a moment where I stupidly thought she might like me and I didn't actually hate the idea, but I wasn't going to tell Banquo that.

"Nevertheless, you knew her best. What might be more important to her?"

And thus began my first lesson with Banquo. And I will admit he was smart, knew his way around the ghostly world, and was generous with his time. But, that doesn't mean I suddenly became one of his disciples, hanging on his every word, kowtowing to him. I listened and I learned.

We tried everything, it took hours and hours. I kept hoping someone would discover the body so we could, at least, get out of that disgusting apartment. But no such luck. The sun set, night passed, and the sun rose before I finally stumbled onto something. It came from fatigue, not thinking.

"Hey, Haley," I said. "You look good today. You know I really appreciate you coming in and helping us out, but I'm kind of torn. I have a policy of not dating any of my staff, and if you weren't... well I would... you know." I used to be an actor, so I sold it. Being all shy and coy, my ghostly cheeks flushing red. I am not sure what possessed me to try it beyond fatigue and what I had learned haunting the office—more than one of the girls and at least one of the boys had had a crush on me.

There was a sharp snap, as the silver cord connecting her spirit to her body broke, her eyes came into focus and a smile formed on her lips. "Doctor Anchor, why, I had no idea." She blinked rapidly a few times, her eyes widening, her mouth opening, her form firming up a bit, looking a little less bardo-ish.

"I couldn't tell you then, Haley," I said, fighting to keep her present. Out of the corner of my eye I saw Banquo beckoning me towards the door, out of the apartment. Yeah, that made sense. Not a good idea for Haley to see her body with the knife sticking out the back and her dried blood looking like reddish-brown cottage cheese. "But now... you know... maybe we can spend some time together."

Her eyes stayed focused on me as we walked through the wall and out of the apartment into the Tucson morning, the sun just peaking over the horizon. "I think I would like that, Doctor Anchor."

Inside I was freaking out—I had no desire for a ghost girlfriend, but I just smiled and held my character. "Haley, it's not Doctor Anchor. It's time you called me Walter."

Chapter Six

THAT DAY I MET EMILY, IN MIDGE'S BATHROOM, THE
bardo so very close, she wore what she calls her "summer
outfit." Blue shorts and a white T-shirt with a drawing of a
red lollipop on it. I stared at her. I hadn't seen a well-
formed ghost before. She looked like a person, just a bit
transparent. The only other ghosts I had run into at the
dental office had been vaporous presences like me.

"You heard me," Emily said. "Leave the lady alone. I
mean it."

My shock and curiosity at seeing her chased the bardo
away. "I… What?" I stammered.

"Christ on a stick, are you a bardo-brained perv or
what?"

"Huh?" I said, not understanding what she was talking
about.

"Did you die in here?" she asked. "Are you going to
spend the rest of eternity haunting people trying to relieve
themselves?"

"No," I said, coming more into myself. "Of course not.

I… I was murdered. She knows something, that letter she just read is a clue."

"Well then, prove it," she said, turned on her heel, and walked through the bathroom door. Something made me follow her. Part of it was that she was a different kind of ghost, part of it was how articulate she was and how young she looked. She spoke with a bit of a lisp making her sound young, yet her words were anything but.

"So," she continued once we were out of the bathroom, "are you trying to be a gumshoe or something?"

I blinked. I knew she was asking if I was a detective, the archaic slang adding to the mystery of her. "I just want to find out who killed me."

"And then what?" she asked, crossing her arms.

"I… well…" I hadn't thought that far.

She shook her head slowly, giving me a most disapproving look. "You don't know anything, do you?" She looked up and added, "Lord, why me? This fellow is so wet behind the ears he's about to drown." She sighed and looked back at me. "Come along. I guess you've won the lottery, big boy, because ole Emily here is going to show you the ropes."

"I need to stay here," I said. "I need to follow Midge. I need to find out who killed me."

She sighed again. "One track mind. Can't say I mind that in a man, as long as the track his mind is on is one I like." She gave me a leering grin that was completely out of place on her young face. "Look… What's your name?"

"Walter."

"Look, Walter. You stay here you will end up in the bardo, a lost cause, a waste of an afterlife. But if you really want to find your killer, come with me now. I'll teach you enough so you can be a proper ghost." With that she walked away. I followed.

Chapter Seven

I KNOW THERE ARE MANY METHODS TO ACTING, BUT there is only one way I know to make my face do what I want it to do: feel the feelings. So if I am playing a part and my character is scared, I do my best to scare myself. It's not the same as a "real" scare—like someone pulling back the shower curtain and lunging at you with a knife—but it's the memory or shadow of the emotion. That's enough.

So my method for acting is... well... Method Acting. I draw on my own past and emotions for the role I am playing. And with Haley, right outside the boring two-story apartment she was murdered in, I was playing the part of suitor. As painful as it was, I summoned the memories of when I courted my ex-wife, that giddy time of being young and falling in love.

Haley was pretty enough—if much too young for me —with high cheek bones, a constellation of freckles perched there, and pale blue eyes. As I talked, her ghostly form came into better focus, but it wasn't great.

I had kept up a patter of flattering talk and gotten her away from the apartment complex and into a little park across the street. It was early morning and except for us ghosts the place was deserted.

"Do you remember?" I asked. The question was intentionally non-specific. I needed info about her murder, but didn't want to push her off the edge back into the bardo.

"What?" she asked, her ghostly form becoming more diffuse.

"It was your eyes, you know," I said, backpedaling. "That light powder blue, they remind me of the sky after a good rainstorm. So lovely."

Her form solidified a bit and her cheeks flushed. "Oh, Doctor Anchor." She saw my stern, but cute, look and added, "I'm sorry... Walter."

"I know," I said, putting a bright smile on my face. "Tell me about your day, tell me everything."

Her eyebrows furrowed, I suspect no man had ever said that to her with such enthusiasm. But I held the expression (and yes, I was acting) and her eyebrows rose and a smile bloomed on her face. She began telling me about her day, every little thing, in exhaustive detail. The girl was obviously starved for attention.

I "um-hummed" in all the right places, asked questions and encouraged details, long before I knew I would need them, and did an Oscar worthy performance hanging on her every word.

It took a while, but when we came to the important information, what she was doing at Roger Coptic's apartment, she had such momentum talking that she didn't seem to notice the bardo-rific territory we had strayed into.

It took everything I had to keep the look of rapt attention on my face when she told me what happened. I wanted to run (or rather, fly) away and give up this whole quest to find my murderer. But I didn't, I held my character and got it all.

Chapter Eight

WHEN EMILY RESCUED ME FROM MIDGE'S BATHROOM, A fact she insisted on telling everyone in the graveyard when I met them, I was a green, wet-behind-the-ears ghost. Emily took me in, kept me out of the bardo, and taught me the basics.

You might think it's easy being a ghost, but you would be wrong, *dead* wrong.

(And if you'd like to laugh, or even clap at the clever use of "dead" in the previous sentence, I won't mind. Actor, remember. I get off on that kind of stuff.)

It is nice to be able to fly, go through walls, not have to eat or bathe. But you trade all that regular human over-head for crushing boredom and the waiting bardo. So as a fresh ghost you have time on your hands (boredom) and way too much time to think about all the mistakes you made in your life, all your regrets, and (in my case) who the hell killed you (that would be the waiting bardo part).

Emily was no gentle teacher, but with eighty years of being a ghost she knew her way around all of that. She taught me and kept me in and around the graveyard for a few months until the day she got tired of me whining (see, I did learn some things from her) and went with me to that apartment where we found Haley with a knife in her back.

HALEY HAD FINALLY LANDED a full-time position at a dental office, so the day she told me about was a day familiar to me. Getting up, doing the mundane activities required to maintain biological life—you know, bathing, eating, eliminating, getting ready to go. It made me nostalgic, because the girl talked about these activities in great detail.

BUT IT WAS HARD FOR ME TO LISTEN TO. DENTISTRY WAS my fallback career but it was still one I enjoyed. And that was fine, but Haley's fulltime job was at Wheeler Dental. As in Doctor Wheeler. As in my former practice partner. As in Haley was working at *my* newly renamed dental office.

Stuff I knew but had effectively repressed after Emily saved me and started helping me be a proper ghost.

I hated the thought, but I smiled and nodded and congratulated her. She had been a fine dental assistant and deserved a full-time gig. Except she wasn't working anywhere anymore, was she? Because she was dead just like me.

And then we got to the good—as in "holy crap"—part.

"Doctor Wheeler asked me to do an errand for him," she said. "As I think back on it now, he seemed a little nervous. He gave me a small package, one of those bubble wrap mailers. It was real light, so it couldn't have had much in it. An address was written on a sticky note, not on the package."

"Did he tell you what was in it?" I asked.

She shrugged her shoulders. "He said I would get paid for the errand, that he would pay overtime. I had done the same thing for Midge a few times before and I needed the money. So..."

So, she didn't care, didn't think to ask.

Now that my memory was coming into clearer focus, I had known that something odd was going on at my office. On my last night alive, Midge had told me she wanted to keep Haley on, which was a surprise. And when I was haunting the office, I had witnessed some of the handling of these packages.

But what does this have to do with my murder? Or Haley's?

"I can see his face so clearly," she continued. "His smile was so big, his teeth so white, but I noticed a bead of sweat on his forehead. And Midge was always a little strange about it too. Super nervous. Sometimes mumbling to herself." She paused, her eyes focusing on me. "It's funny that I can remember things so clearly. My memory has always been a little poor, but not today. I can remember my first day of high school as clear as a bell. Want to hear about it?"

"I would love to hear about it," I said, making sure the smile on my face was not too big. "But, let's finish up with the day you are telling me about already. Okay?"

She nodded.

"What was the address on the package?"

She kind-of walked towards the swing set as she rattled off the address to Roger Coptic's apartment. Her walk was most definitely a "kind-of." While her form was better than it previously was, she still looked positively ghostly with a vague movement of her legs as she floated over the green grass towards the little swing set. It takes practice, a lot of it, to look fully human.

"Do you remember what happened when you delivered it?" I knew she did. She was clearly experiencing the enhanced memory that we ghosts have. Funny, we are all literally brainless and yet have a nearly eidetic memory.

"The little man that answered the door scared me. He hadn't shaved in a few days and his teeth were stained yellow. I handed him the package and he smiled at me. He had a missing tooth." She pointed to her mouth, tooth number ten, the right lateral incisor. It was really bad form for her to be so vague, considering our former business. "He invited me in. I didn't want to go in, but he insisted, saying he had to get something for me to return to Doctor Wheeler. I stood there holding the package, smelling the rotting garbage smell of the place when…" She stopped, her form going diffuse, her eyes getting wide.

"What?" I asked.

"I… My…" she stammered, her right arm vaguely pointing towards her back where she had been stabbed. "Pain. It hurt so much. I cried out. I fell. Someone took the package out of my hand."

"Did you see him?" I asked.

She shook her head. "But he had nice shoes. All black and polished and old fashioned. Like the dads wear in those movies about the fifties."

Well, that explained the chanting of "Blaaaack Shooooes" when we found her. "What happened then, Haley?" I knew she was on a one-way ticket to bardo-land, but kept pushing. I needed to know what she knew.

"Then I saw that man's face, the one that answered the door, with his scraggly beard and his horrible breath. It smelled like old cigarettes and rotten cheese. He was freaking out, cursing, and then I was alone. It got so cold… it hurt so much…"

The girl was definitely losing it. I caught Banquo looking at me, his little nod and widening eyes making it clear he wanted me to do something about it, that he didn't want to see her bardoed again.

"What happened to me? So cold…" she muttered.

Emily was staring at me too, her arms crossed, her little hip cocked. Her body language said, "I helped you, you've got to help her."

So I did the only thing I could think of. I fell back into the role I had been playing and I kissed her.

Chapter Nine

BEING A GHOST, THE RULES ARE DIFFERENT. EVERY ONCE in a while things happen that remind me just how different they are. Like when I kissed Haley in that little park across from where she was killed.

Touching as a ghost takes a lot of skill. Emily had taught it to me when she was showing me the ropes. She thought it essential to my survival (and even though ghostly touching is a shadow of what it is like when you're alive, imagine an existence without it). And besides, Emily likes to high-five. Well, with us it's more of a high five for her and a low five for me.

Okay, so ghosts can walk through walls and, really, walk through anything—even other ghosts. So there are two components to ghostly touching: matching frequency and intent. The frequency part is about making your ghostly form the same as the ghost you want to touch. In this case that meant me becoming a diffuse almost-bardoed mess. I was trying to make what passed for our lips come together.

Back at the graveyard, Jim and Jane are a couple, but

they don't seem to be into public displays of affection, so I was going in blind.

When our lips met, what happened was not what I expected. I felt our lips touch, the numb sense of ghostly touch, but then…

I felt my body, weak and cold, with the hard floor underneath me. I smelled the musty, grimy carpet. I saw the slick, old-fashioned black shoes, a well-manicured hand taking the package, and the person leaving. I saw the gap-toothed grin of Roger Coptic and smelled his rotten breath. And then I was alone and so cold. I couldn't move, I couldn't speak. I realized that I was dying, that the pain in my back was killing me. I worried about my mother, we were supposed to go to the movies tonight. I worried about my cat, who was going to feed him? I thought of a man I had once loved. But then, even my thoughts became less coherent. I felt confused and upset and knew death was close, ready to take me.

The sequence of senses and thoughts restarted and played over and over again. I was stuck in Haley's death, feeling what she felt, thinking what she thought.

"All right, all right," a high-pitched voice said. "Break it up kids. I mean, really, get a room." I heard it dimly as if it was coming from a great distance. But it distracted me from the death scene I was reliving. "Seriously, you two. Break it up or I'm going to get physical with you."

I couldn't do anything about what was happening. I was lost, stuck, sliding into the bardo with Haley.

"Okay, don't say I didn't warn you," Emily said. I felt this sharp sensation in my foot. I can't call it pain, but it got my attention, and then I was standing right in front of Haley, her eyes wide.

"Doctor Anchor," Haley whispered, her hand going to

her face. Her form looked better, less ghost-ish and more human-ish, actually much better than it had.

I looked down at my own form and I was the diffuse mess. Emily was standing right next to me shaking her head. "Kids these days," she said, and marched back to Banquo who had a bemused look on his face. I concentrated on my own form until it came into focus. I was wearing my usual post-death outfit. Actually it was my usual pre-death outfit: scrubs. As a dentist I had practically lived in them, it is what came naturally.

"Are you okay, Haley?" I asked.

She nodded and gave me a smile. It is the kind of smile Emily would call "come hither." It was clear that my experience kissing her had been different than hers. When I talked about ghosts touching, I mentioned intent. Well, my intent had been to keep her out of the bardo, and somehow I had taken on part of her death burden and done that, but nearly went to bardo-land myself.

"Are you okay, Doctor Anchor?" she asked. I was most definitely out of character. I am sure the wide variety of emotions I had been feeling had been all over my face.

"Please, Haley," I said, pulling the tatters of my role back on, just as I had pulled my ghostly form together. "You must call me Walter. I think we are far past the point where you need to call me Doctor." I offered her my arm, modulating it for touch and having a clear intent to *just* touch. She took it and we walked away from the park and towards the graveyard.

It would take us most of the day to walk there, but it gave me time. Time to get her oriented. Time to help her understand that she was dead. Time for me to find out if Haley knew anything else that might lead to her murderer and mine.

Chapter Ten

Doctor Elias Wheeler and I became very close after that. Haley, as it turns out, didn't know anything else. Doctor Wheeler had had her deliver a package to Roger Coptic. She was murdered. Someone took the package. Roger fled.

Wheeler—I am going to drop the "Doctor"; it's a sign of respect, something I no longer have for him—was under our surveillance. And by "our" I mean me, Emily, and Haley.

For the first few weeks it was either Emily or myself watching him, while the other stayed with Haley at the graveyard, helping her adjust to being a ghost. After that it was all three of us. Once Haley started getting comfortable as a ghost, she got mad.

"Haley's gone comet," Emily whispered to me. I had come back to the graveyard for our shift change. Emily was on her way into the mortuary, a ritual where the ghosts check out the newly dead that is called the "greeting committee." Wheeler was asleep and it was a safe time to do it.

"What?" I asked.

"You know, Haley's Comet. The girl is on fire, lit up, burning across the sky—"

"Emily, can you please just tell me what's going on and stop with the metaphors."

Emily rolled her eyes and stuck her tongue out at me. "Spoil sport. The girl is pissed. She's angry. She's ready to rip Wheeler's heart out and eat it for breakfast. She is the proverbial woman scorned. She—"

"Okay, okay," I said, cutting her off and holding my hands up. "I get it. She wants revenge."

A wicked smile crept onto Emily's lips. "Which brings us to your planned breakup."

I had continued on with my "relationship" with Haley. It wasn't that big of a deal. We spent time together, held hands, and kissed here and there. When she got into troubling territory, kissing seemed to calm her down, ground her, and I had gotten better at not taking too much on from her. I had told Emily that I planned to break it off as soon as she got stabilized. I liked the girl, had grown quite fond of her—I just didn't want to carry on a relationship that I had started out of desperation.

"You think…" I began.

"Didn't you hear what I said about 'woman scorned'?" Emily asked.

"Where is she?"

"She's talking with Banquo," Emily said, her voice rising half an octave when she said his name. "I refused to give her any haunting tips, so she sought him out."

"As if he'll help her with that," I said with a chuckle.

"As if I was going to tell her *that* in the mood she was in," Emily shot back.

We stood there silently. I was lost in my thoughts, frankly dismayed at what I had gotten myself into. "I'm sure she'll understand," I finally said. "I mean, I kissed her to save her from the bardo."

Emily snorted and shook her head. "Look, Walter, you kissed her so you could get what you wanted and just happened to save her from the bardo. I may have died when I was four, but even I know you don't mess with a woman's heart." She chuckled softly. "Especially not a woman like that."

I really do hate being dead sometimes.

Emily walked away and left me there to stew. I looked around. Ghosts were rising out of the ground, flying, or popping in, gathering in small groups around gravestones. Midnight was approaching, we all could feel it. Midnight is our time, when we ghosts feel most "alive."

I didn't stay long. That night the surveillance became the three of us. And let me tell you, you've never been surveilled until you've been surveilled by ghosts. There is nothing you can do, nothing you can say, nowhere you can go that we can't follow you, can't hear you, can't know what you are doing.

We were brutal—the man got no privacy at all. Emily even insisted that we follow him into the bathroom, and that is where things got interesting.

Chapter Eleven

ELIAS WHEELER IS A YOUNG, COCKY DENTIST, WITH A shaved head, overly bleached white teeth, and a chubby face. He is also much more of a salesman than I ever was. It's one of the reasons I had brought him into the practice three years ago. He was eager to get out there and bring new clients in, he had energy for that. I didn't anymore.

I have never trusted people in sales. They have an ulterior motive—their own profit—so how can you trust what they are saying? They are worse than actors in my book. At least sometimes us actors aren't playing a role.

"I don't want to watch him take another dump," I complained to Emily. Wheeler had just gone into his bathroom in his lovely ranch-style home, in what would likely be another long session. He's got IBS or some other kind of issue, because he spends a lot of time in there.

"Too bad," Emily said. "I am young and innocent and shouldn't be subject to such indignities, and you wouldn't make your girlfriend watch another man defecate."

I sighed and nodded, heading for the bathroom,

pondering how Emily had found me in a bathroom but refused to watch Wheeler there.

"And who said chivalry is dead?" Emily offered as I walked through the bathroom door.

I can't tell you how sick of Elias Wheeler I was. His every little habit annoyed the hell out of me. Singing in the shower, checking all the locks on the doors two times before going to bed, the three girlfriends he was stringing along while setting up several more on online dating sites. But while he seemed to be a contemptible human being, we hadn't turned up a single clue in the ten days we had been haunting—I mean surveilling—him.

As he sat on his porcelain throne, his jeans down to his ankles, playing some stupid game on his iPhone, it rang. And horror of horrors, he answered. That's right, in the middle of an extensive toileting event, he answered his phone. No class whatsoever.

I didn't see the caller ID, I wasn't positioned correctly —and I should have been. It only rang once and he put it to his ear.

"Wheeler," he said.

He bit his lip as he listened and nodded his head a few times, the color draining from his face. "Look, we had a deal. I've orchestrated your deliveries. I don't—"

Belatedly I maneuvered my ghostly head right next to Wheeler's fleshy one so I could hear both sides of the conversation. I normally did better than this, but I think time and the whole "bathroom" part of this had thrown me off my game.

"...release the photos, but I will," a female voice said. "You are in deep, my friend, and the only way out is through."

"Look," he said, licking his lips and sitting up straighter on the toilet. "Someone died last time I had a package

34

delivered for you. That wasn't what was supposed to happen."

"I told you, we weren't expecting the intensity of our competitor's interest. We've taken precautions. It won't happen again."

Wheeler sighed. "This has got to end," he said.

"It will," the voice on the phone said. "I promise, it will end soon." There was a brief pause and then she added, "The package will be at drop point three. See that it is delivered promptly."

WHEN WHEELER and I finally got out of the bathroom, the last thing I thought I'd be feeling was empathy for the fellow. After that phone call, he appeared to be a victim too.

As we all stood in the kitchen watching him nervously eat some cereal, I brought Emily and Haley up to speed.

"He... he wasn't trying to hurt me?" Haley asked.

"No, darling," I replied, still playing the role of the dutiful detective-boyfriend. "He appears to be a pawn in this thing."

She nodded mutely, staring at Wheeler.

"Don't get all misty-eyed there, Haley-Bopp," Emily said. "This still doesn't make him a shining example of the human race. He's done things he's ashamed of; the blackmailers are using that against him."

"Right," I interjected, trying to get things back on track. "We'll follow him to the drop point. Emily, you will stay there and see if the blackmailers come back. Haley and I will stick with Wheeler and follow him to the delivery and track the package from there."

And that is what we did. On the way to work, Wheeler stopped by Freedom Park north of the air force base and pulled a package from under a park bench. Emily stayed there and we followed Wheeler who went to the office and talked another young girl into delivering a package for him. Her name was Rachel, she was even younger and more innocent-looking than Haley.

"I don't have a good feeling about this," Haley said.

I nodded. At this point I never had a good feeling in the dental offices. It reminded me too much of the life I once had, the life I had lost. I mean, it hadn't been much, but it had been mine. I looked at Haley and wondered if she would kiss me if I started to lose it and go bardo.

"Stay with Rachel," I told Haley. I really didn't want to split us up, but I didn't think we were done with Wheeler yet.

She nodded, her eyes wide. We had hardly been apart since I had gotten her out of the bardo.

"It's okay, Haley. I won't leave the office without you. If you run into trouble, just come find me."

She bit her lip, her eyes lingering on me for a moment before she turned and followed Rachel.

I stayed with Wheeler. I was sure there was something else to be learned from him.

Chapter Twelve

IN SOME WAYS THE KIND OF SCRUTINY WE WERE GIVING Wheeler wasn't fair. No human that is watched that much turns out looking pretty. People have their oddities, their addictions, their weaknesses. Wheeler was no exception. He picked his nose, stared at ladies' asses when they weren't looking, and liked to look at himself in the mirror.

But that is all I found out about him as I watched him go about his job, my former job, doing dental exams, fillings, root planing—all the joys of dentistry. It was a hard day for me. As much as I have grown to dislike Wheeler, I was jealous of him that he was alive.

Just after 5:00 p.m., Haley came and got me. Rachel was leaving. I looked back at Wheeler as we left. There was something else there, something important. I just knew it.

Rachel was skinny and tall, with short blonde hair and a quick walk. She left with the package Wheeler had picked up in the morning, got in her little red Hyundai, and drove to the Park Mall on Broadway. She did a lot of window shopping as she darted from store to store.

"Is she shopping?" Haley asked. "What the hell is she doing?"

I shrugged and we kept following her. She stopped at every clothing store in the mall and finally went into Spencer's. You know, the place with all the goofy stuff like drinking and sex games, odd clothing, and kinkier stuff. Haley gave me a look. I shrugged and we followed her in.

Rachel went right to the counter and asked for George. The overly perky checkout girl went into the back and out came George. He was thirtyish, overweight, and (I would wager) under-dated. He had greasy brown hair and wire-rimmed glasses.

"Are you George?" Rachel asked.

The big guy just nodded.

"This is for you," she said handing over the package and walking out of the store. George grunted and went into the back of the store, we followed.

The back room was what you would expect. Small and crowded with boxes, cleaning supplies, and a cramped desk. George sat at the desk and ripped opened the package, licking his lips like he hadn't eaten for days and this was a juicy steak he was tearing into.

He pulled out a small rectangular piece of plastic.

"That's a micro SD card," Haley said.

I looked at her. "A what?"

She rolled her eyes, looking back at George. "A memory chip for your computer. There's data on it."

Post-divorce, I had dated a few younger women, and even though Haley and I were both dead, she had just managed to make me feel old. It is not a pleasant feeling, a twisting in your guts. The young don't understand—as you get older, sure your body feels different, but no matter your age you feel like *you*. In my experience, it's the world that makes you feel old. The changing times, changing activities, and the attitude like Haley had just had.

The youth do not treat older people like we treat them. Think of children, people older than them are patient and understanding of their ignorance. The young do not tend to show the same tolerance for ignorance in people older than them.

I didn't say a thing, though. I kept my mouth shut and watched as George plugged the card into his computer and tapped on the keyboard.

Haley narrated what he was doing—she made an assumption that because I hadn't recognized a micro SD card without any labeling that I didn't know anything about computers. Which wasn't exactly true, but close enough. I was, though, grateful that the eye rolling had ended.

"The data is compressed and encrypted," she said. "He's entering the encrypting key…" She watched him carefully as he typed, he had to do it a couple of times to get it right. "The password is 'GetRichGeorge**$$.' Okay, he's got it unpacked. It's a bunch of files… there's some source code. He's compiling it. Now he's running it. Oh…"

She trailed off, I could see for myself as the screen lit up with a still of tanks and soldiers and explosions, with "Warmonger II" emblazoned on it.

Haley went diffuse as she watched as George briefly played the game. I didn't say anything.

"Holy shit," George said to himself. "This is the real goddam deal. I'm gonna be rich!"

Haley was sliding towards the bardo. "A video game?" she said, looking at me. "I was killed for a video game? What the hell kind of world is this?"

I had a brief, stabbing moment of empathy. What if I had been killed over something mundane or trivial? Did I really want to know? What kind of difference would it make?

"Walter?" she said, her voice cracking, her powder blue eyes way too wide. "Why?" She looked back at George as he continued to tap away at the computer.

I thought of kissing her again, the first time I had seemed to take on some of her fear and stabilized her. But that wasn't the right thing to do for her long-term, she needed to learn to calm herself. I modulated my form to match hers and took her face in my hands.

"Look at me," I said, her eyes reluctantly leaving George. They were still too wide, but she stopped getting more diffuse. "Listen to me, Haley. Focus on my voice. You are strong enough to do this. It doesn't matter why you were killed, but I promise you, I will find who did it and find a way to make them pay."

I was a bit taken aback by my tone. I sounded fierce and protective. I sounded strong and sure of myself. I sounded like I cared about her. And, actually, I wasn't acting. Something changed in that moment. I wasn't off farting around trying to do something for myself. I now had a mission, a purpose beyond my own needs.

Haley blinked, her form coming back into focus. I kept my hands on her face, matching them to her form as she changed. Tears rolled down her cheeks and she slowly nodded and licked her lips.

"I need you, Haley," I said. Her eyes grew wide again, but for a different reason. "I need you to be strong. I need your help. I can't do this without you."

She leaned in and kissed me. It wasn't like a flesh kiss, we didn't have "lips" per se. It wasn't about a physical sensation. It was what was left over. Passion. Communication. Communion.

I lost myself to that kiss and gave her back everything I

could. It was like we spoke volumes to each other in those moments. It was like falling off a cliff, or riding a rocket, or losing your mind. With the flesh aspects gone, the spiritual aspects of it were multiplied.

I don't know how long it lasted, it's like time didn't matter there, but when it was done I was changed. No more acting. Haley *was* my girlfriend. I felt this relief well up in me—all those lonely years I had experienced when I was alive were over.

Our faces only inches apart, she smiled broadly and I smiled back.

She looked around, her eyes growing wide again. "Oh shit," she said. "Where did he go?"

Chapter Thirteen

WE COULDN'T FIND HIM. THAT BREAK IN OUR FOCUS had given George enough time to get away from us. We searched the mall. We searched the parking lot. We searched and searched until night came and midnight approached.

The search after the first hour had been useless. I had known it, but Haley was upset and seemed to need to keep looking.

"He'll be back," I said. "We can just go back to the store and wait for him."

She sighed and nodded.

"But, I don't think it matters. We should go back to the graveyard, catch the Midnight Circle, and then rest."

"What?" She shook her head, looking confused. Now that the whole "you died for a video game" thing was known, she was holding on even tighter to finding her killer.

"George doesn't matter. He didn't kill you. I've been thinking about it. We've got a seller, the one blackmailing Wheeler, a buyer, George, and a third party—your killer."

She was staring at me now, her blue eyes flashing. I was glad to see anger instead of despair. We floated just above the parking lot of the mall, a bland expanse of pavement mostly devoid of cars at this hour.

"We need to find the third party. George can't help with that. The seller might be able to."

She nodded. I was glad I was making sense, because I was just working it out as I spoke.

"We left Emily at the package drop-off. Let's go see if she found something out."

Haley nodded slowly and then came close to me. "Thank you," she whispered and she kissed me again.

I have to say, we were getting better at this, and once again, no acting. I was falling for this girl and hard.

Chapter Fourteen

"You're disgusting," Emily said to the homeless man sleeping on the bench we had left her at. "Don't you care? Thank God we ghosts can't smell, because I'm sure your scent would make me vomit. Look, I know life is hard. I know it can just mow you down. But, really, wake up. Get your act together. Do something worth doing. You are alive, for God's sake. Do you know what kind of gift that is? And here you are passed out drunk on a park bench with your dirty clothes and your scraggly beard. You're wasting that gift. Don't you have family? A mother, a father, a child, someone that cares for you, someone that needs you?" Emily paused, taking a deep breath. "Find the strength to make something of your life. Please. You've got one. I never did, I..."

Haley and I had taken our time getting back to the park. We had talked and held hands and kissed—and in general acted like people falling in love. When we entered Freedom Park and saw Emily, we both stopped without a word and listened. As her soliloquy went on, I began to feel guilty, but I couldn't bring myself to do anything about it.

She eventually noticed us, and stopped mid-sentence, a blush of red springing to her chubby cheeks.

"What the hell are you looking at?" she yelled.

"I... We..." I stammered. In our relationship, Emily had been the strong one (expect for the occasional four-year-old fit). Her being jealous of a drunk, homeless man wasn't something I had been expecting.

"Useless damn day," she said, looking down at her little feet. "Nothing happened here. I..." Emily's face clouded up and she took a few steps towards us. "I was just..." she began, looking back at the homeless man. "I think sometimes we can get through. You know, be the 'still small voice' that helps people turn it around. Be..."

Tears started to roll down her face. I let go of Haley's hand and went to her. I modulated my form to hers and took her in my arms. She held me tightly and cried for the longest time. This was no four-year-old fit, this was a ghost's grief. We all feel it. We aren't "alive" anymore. We barely exist in this world. The only thing we really have is each other.

I forgot Haley and gave Emily my full attention. I held her and whispered to her and let her get it all out. For the first time in our relationship, she really needed me.

When it was all over, I looked around and Haley was gone.

Chapter Fifteen

IT DIDN'T TAKE LONG TO FIND HALEY. SHE STOOD IN
Roger Coptic's apartment staring at a reddish-brown stain
on the floor. The place she had died. They had finally
taken the body away and there had been yellow crime
scene tape over the door.

"Haley…" I said softly. Her form wasn't in very good
shape, and I was afraid she was lost to the bardo.

"What kind of life is this?" she asked.

I didn't know if she was referring to her murder and
her physical life or her ghostly afterlife. "The only one
we've got," I answered, covering both possibilities.

She looked up at me pursing her lips and nodding. "It
doesn't seem like enough."

I approached her, leaving Emily by the door. I
extended my hand to her and said, "Please. Come."

She ignored my gesture, her gaze returning to the
blood stain. "I didn't do anything wrong. I didn't deserve
this."

"No, you didn't," I said, putting my hand on her shoulder. She let my hand stay there, not moving, not speaking, just staring at the stain.

Finally she looked up at me, her eyes hard and unwavering. "We are going to find who did this. I don't care how long it takes. And then I'm going to make his life a living hell."

I stepped back, my hand leaving her shoulder. I was scared. Emily had been silent this whole time, but I heard her gasp as I backed away. Haley wasn't close to going bardo. She was somewhere else, somewhere very different.

"Okay," I said. It sounded empty next to her fierceness.

"What's our next lead?" she asked.

"I don't know," I answered.

"That's not good enough."

"I know." My answer sounded hollow, like I was whispering into a hurricane. Haley now seemed like a force of nature. You don't let down a force of nature. I racked my brain trying to think.

A gaming black market. Buyers and sellers. A third party that killed Haley and stole the product. We found one of the buyers, but that's it.

I looked around the grubby apartment of Roger Coptic. I ignored Haley as best I could, but I could feel her eyes on me as I studied the place. A sink full of dirty dishes. Overflowing garbage. Dirty clothing all over the bedroom. A cracked flat-screen TV. No computer in sight.

"Whoever Roger Coptic is, he wasn't the buyer," I said, desperate to fill the silence.

"Who was he, then?" Emily asked. I was so glad she had stepped in. Emily is as tough as they come, but Haley's shift from scared love interest to avenging ghost had shocked even her.

"I am guessing he was a middleman," I said. I thought

it all over, trying to connect the clues we had found. "I
don't think this is just about video games."

"What? Why?" Haley asked.

"Both Doctor Wheeler and Midge are involved. Midge
for money and they have something on Wheeler. They've
done this before, moving things. It can't always be video
games." I paused, thinking it over again. "I think this is
about industrial espionage. Trade secrets."

Haley nodded. "That SD card had the source code to
the video game. That's valuable, and using the old-fashioned sneaker-net may be more secure these days than the
Internet."

"Great," Emily said. "So what the hell do we do now?"

"I'm guessing that since a murder occurred here, Roger
is not coming back. He's probably on the run. He must
know something."

"Then we find him," Haley said.

"How?" I asked.

Emily caught my eye and then pointedly looked at
Haley. I gave Emily a nod and sighed. It was the only way.

"You're a ghost," Emily began, walking over to Haley
and looking up at her. "You saw him. If you really want to
find him, nothing in this world can stop you."

"I don't know what you mean," Haley said.

"It's generally called 'popping,'" I said, "because of the
sound a ghost makes when they appear or disappear. You
can travel from point to point at will."

"Like this," Emily said. She was standing next to me,
her face going blank, and then she was gone with a soft
"pop." A moment later there was another "pop" and she
was standing next to Haley.

"How..." Haley began.

"It's kind of an advanced skill," I said. "Not one that

I've acquired yet, but Emily here is very good at it. She can teach you."

Emily nodded. "But not here. Let's get back to the graveyard. This is going to take some time."

As Emily and I floated towards the door, Haley said, "Wait." We both turned and looked at her. "If I can do this, then why don't I just 'pop' to my murderer? I saw those old-fashioned shoes."

"That's not enough," Emily said. "You'd probably end up in a shoe store or shoe factory or someone's closet. A face, though. That is unique. That will work."

EMILY TRIED to get Banquo to help teach us how to pop. Since the teaching was going to happen, I was determined to learn too. But Banquo would have nothing of it once he learned what Haley intended. And it's not like Haley was keeping it to herself. She came right out and told him when he asked her why she wanted to learn. The phrase "make his life a living hell" put a most sour expression on Banquo's face.

Haley was different and I missed her. My affection had become real, and then she became this avenging spirit. No more displays of affection, no more long talks, just a single-minded focus. Find Roger Coptic.

I did, though, find a use for my acting skills. I spent the next several weeks while Emily taught us acting like it didn't bother me that things had changed.

But they had and it did.

Eventually Haley "popped" and we found Roger

Coptic. He was dead, and that turned out to be our big
break in the case.

Chapter Sixteen

THE SAYING "DEAD MEN DON'T TALK" NEEDS TO BE rethought. Roger Coptic sang, he sang like a bird.

When Haley finally popped, both Emily and I were surprised. It had been days of frustrating, never ending attempts. And then, finally, she was gone. Emily grabbed my hand and popped us to her. And there we found Roger Coptic.

His body was on the ground next to a dumpster behind a Denny's, the head at an unnatural angle. Roger's spirit was hovering above it, a thin silver cord snaking from the body to the spirit.

He hadn't been dead long—usually ghosts figure out how to sever the cord pretty quickly. This is the first initiation into the ghostly afterlife.

"Who killed me?" Haley asked Roger, her voice loud and strident.

First recognition bloomed on Roger's face and then confusion. "What? You... you're dead."

"Who killed me?" Haley repeated.

Roger's eyes darted around, he still looked confused.

"I'm angry," she said. "I'm sure you can see that. You help me, I walk away. You don't help me and I take out my anger on you."

Both Emily and I took a step back; Haley's form was flickering red along the edges. I looked down at her and saw fear on Emily's face. Ghosts can go bad just like people.

"Yeah... yeah... sure," Roger began, his eyes wide, his hands up. He backed up until his body was halfway into the brick wall of the Denny's. "What the..." His head swiveled around and his diffuse limbs flayed. He didn't know he was dead. He didn't understand he was a ghost. Such confusion is very common.

"Talk. Now," Haley said. "Or it will only get worse."

"Right... yeah... The dude's name is Halifax. He's the one that stole the delivery. He hurt me too. Said he was tying up loose ends. He..." Roger looked down and saw his body, his mouth going wide and his form diffusing even more.

"Where can I find this Halifax?" Haley yelled at Roger, getting his attention.

"He's here," Roger said, his head nodding towards the restaurant. "After we talked, he said he was hungry."

Haley gave him a sharp nod and began flying around the building. She was still a new ghost, a practiced one would have just flown through the wall. I looked at Emily.

"You stop her," she said, "before she does..." Emily sighed. "If she does what I'm afraid she'll do, you know where it will end up for her. I'll handle the little guy, see what else he knows."

I nodded and flew after Haley. I got in front of her before she got to the door.

"What are you going to do, Haley?" I asked.

"Out of my way, Walter," she said.

52

"This won't end well."

"No it won't," she said, a grim look on her face. "But it will end."

I kept myself in front of her, blocking the door. This went on for a minute or so before she sighed and walked right through me.

It was early afternoon and the Denny's wasn't very crowded. It didn't take long to find the man with the black shoes; they were pointy, cap toe Oxfords. He was eating waffles and drinking coffee.

He was meticulously groomed and wore a shirt, jacket, and tie. He ate with a slow precision. Cutting a piece of the waffle. Putting down his knife. Using the fork to put the food in his mouth. Putting down his fork. Chewing slowly and thoroughly. Taking a sip of coffee and resuming the process.

He seemed to take great pleasure in it.

Haley stood staring at him, her hands shaking, tears running down her cheeks. The red flickering along her form had turned to crimson, making her rage abundantly clear. She kept looking at his shoes. They were indeed the same as the ones I saw when I first kissed her and experienced her death. There was no doubt that this was her killer.

"Let's follow him and get his name and address," I said softly. "We can then go to the SECI chamber and let someone know. They can tell the police." SECI stands for the Search for Extracorporeal Intelligence. A project started at the University of Arizona to allow the dead to communicate with the living. This is what JJ Lynch used to write his memoir. It is what I am using now to write this story. Haley knew about it, I was just reminding her.

She shook her head slowly, her nostrils flaring. "That's not enough." She turned and looked at me. The look on her face made me want to take a step back, but I held my ground, keeping my face passive. "He's a killer. He has to die. He deserves to die."

I didn't tell her, but in principle I agreed, although I preferred someone locking him up and throwing away the key. Killing him didn't sit well with me, but then again I wasn't the one he murdered. If I was looking at my own killer I would probably want the same thing. "If you kill him," I said, "he could become one of us."

"And then I'll find ways to make his afterlife a living hell," she said, turning back to him.

Can a ghost kill a person? It's not easy, but it is possible. If the stories are to be believed, JJ Lynch did it. There are whispers that if you have the right focus and modulate your form correctly, you might be able to make someone trip or look away at the wrong moment when they are driving. There is even darker talk of possession.

"You might not want to stay around for this," she said.

"Sorry, you can't get rid of me that easily."

She glanced at me and shrugged and began her haunting. She went at it like she had a plan, like she knew what she was doing, like she knew that it would work. This puzzled me. How could she know what to do? I didn't and I had been dead a lot longer than her.

They say that "hell hath no fury like a woman scorned." Well, try a ghost confronting her murderer. Haley got her head close to Halifax, who was seated comfortably at a booth table, and started speaking to him. Her tone low, she spoke quickly, and didn't stop. She kept up a nonstop diatribe against him. "You are worthless. You would be better off dead. How can you stand yourself? Do the world a favor and stab yourself in the throat with that fork. You don't deserve to be alive." And on it went. It was as if she was playing the part of that negative voice we all have in our heads. The one that doubts us. The one that wonders whether we are worth the space we take up.

"What the hell is she doing?" Emily asked. The man had finished his breakfast and paid. Emily found us in the parking lot as he got into his vintage Cadillac.

"I think she's trying to talk him to death." I said it with a grin, but my attempt at humor fell flat. "I think she's trying to get into his head. Get him to do something to himself."

Emily sighed as we flew into the car with Haley and the man. "She's been talking to some of the ghosts over by the crypts."

"What?" I asked.

"I spotted her there a few days back. I didn't say anything… I was hopeful she wouldn't go this way."

At our graveyard some of the more disturbed and dangerous ghosts live by and in the crypts. Most of them are in the bardo, but kind of violent—they'll lash out at any ghost (or person) that comes too close to them. And there are other ghosts that choose to stay there that are into the darker aspects of what you can do as a ghost.

"Why didn't you tell me?" I asked.

"I could see you were getting attached… I…" Tears welled up in Emily's eyes. She was going all four-year-old on me and I couldn't be mad at her. "I'm sorry, Walter. Can you ever forgive me?"

I gave her a hug and said, "Of course. We'll get through this." I sounded confident, but I was far from it.

Chapter Seventeen

As far as hauntings go, things that go bump in the night are no big deal. Furious murder victims that unleash an unending soul sucking tirade on you... well, that's a whole 'nother story.

We tried everything (short of touching her) to get Haley's attention. She was oblivious to us. And we didn't try touching because of what I had learned when I kissed her the first time. It's possible to take on some of the emotional content of another ghost with that kind of intimacy, and I didn't want to take on what she was giving.

Haley's technique seemed to refine. She floated behind her victim, her furious face recognizable and her arms visible, but the rest of her diffuse and vaporous. She ended up with her fingers stuck into the guy's temples and slowly refined her screed.

"You are a worthless human being. You should do the world a favor and kill yourself. Right now. What do you have to live for? Your life is an unending torment. Pick up the knife, go ahead. Look how sharp that blade is. Just pull it across your throat and this will all be over."

It was starting to get to me, and Emily had this pinched look on her round face. But we stayed with Haley and followed them as the man drove to a beautiful little house that bordered the Catalina Mountains north of Tucson. As he went about his day, checking his email, typing on the computer, paying bills, swimming in the pool, dusting and vacuuming.

Haley's diatribe seemed to be having an effect. He started rubbing at his temples and stretching his neck. He took some Advil and he tried to take a nap.

The man's name is Edgar Halifax, and as far as solving Haley's murder, and many others, we had him. That typing he did on his computer? He documented, in exacting detail, the murder of Roger Coptic. He had a diary of everyone he had killed, whether it was contract or personal and how much he was paid. Roger's murder was on contract, part of the one that involved him stealing what Haley was carrying.

The man was meticulous in his dress, how he kept his home, and in documenting his work. We also watched closely as he typed his password. It's "GardenState32#!." My guess is he's from New Jersey.

I didn't feel good about it, though—solving the murder, that is. Haley was unreachable, inconsolable, incoherent, and raging. Emily's jokes earlier about Haley's Comet and Haley-Bopp now seemed unnerving and prescient.

"This is no 'small still voice.' This is…" Emily said after about five hours of this, her face pained. We were in his kitchen, all gleaming steel and granite countertops, watching him prepare his dinner in his ultra-meticulous fashion.

"We're in over our heads," I said. "Go get Banquo."

Her eyes got wide and she nodded her head quickly a few times and with a "pop" was gone.

"Haley," I said, trying one more time to reach her. "Please stop this. Please. Can't we go back a few steps? I... I thought maybe we had something there. I thought maybe this life had gotten less lonely for me. I thought maybe, just maybe, I had found something that had eluded me when I was alive."

You may be wondering if I was acting. I wasn't. Her eyes found mine and her diatribe stopped.

"Please, Haley. Can we just talk? I just want to have a conversation."

Her brows furrowed and she blinked, her eyes holding mine. The look on her face tore my heart out. Her bottom lip quivered as if she was trying to speak. Her eyes spoke clearly of pain and regret. A single tear ran down her cheek. She then turned back to Edgar and resumed her soliloquy.

I turned away. Not because I didn't want her to see me cry, but because I knew part of her wanted me and that part was not in charge. She wasn't the Haley I had grown fond of. She knew exactly what she was doing and the terrible price she would have to pay.

I turned away because I didn't know how to stop her... or rather didn't have the courage to try the only thing left to try.

Chapter Eighteen

BANQUO CAN BE ARROGANT AND DEMANDING. HE CAN BE short with people and doesn't suffer fools. When Emily finally came back with him, he was none of these things.

The night had passed and Edgar was having breakfast. Meticulous little bites of his poached eggs and toast. He sat at the little breakfast nook in his kitchen that overlooked the formal Zen garden in his backyard. But he looked different. He was harried, black circles under his eyes.

"Thank God you're here," I said when I saw Banquo.

Banquo nodded and gave me a small compassionate smile. He strode over to Haley and Edgar and stood for a long time staring at them.

"Sorry," Emily whispered. "He was otherwise engaged. I had to wait."

I looked at Emily and nodded. I caught a view of my own form and found that I had gone pretty diffuse myself. Edgar was not the only one getting worn down by this. "Did he say anything?"

"Not much. He's worried." Emily's awe for Banquo

was still fully intact, but the girlish crush was gone. He was our best hope and we both knew it.

Banquo paced around the two of them, walking right through the little table. His eyes had this faraway look to them as he stared at Haley and Edgar. Banquo kept walking and then holding still and then walking again. At one point he most tentatively touched Haley's form, but quickly removed his finger like it stung.

Finally he moved to Emily and me and said, "This way." He flew straight up and out of the house.

I would have told him I didn't want to leave Haley. But he was gone and then Emily, so I followed.

"How long has she been like this?" he asked once we were atop the ceramic shingled roof.

"About twenty hours," I said. He was looking at me, not at Emily.

"And how invested are you in her recovery?"

I blinked and looked to Emily. Her green eyes were wide and kind, but not helpful. "Umm… very. I'm very invested in her recovery."

He nodded. "Then you know what to do and you know how risky it is."

"How…" I began.

He shook his head, moving it a minute distance to the left and the right. "Not a useful question."

Here he was: terse, teaching, demanding Banquo. One of the reasons I wasn't a big fan of his, but I needed him.

"Can you explain the risk? I'm not sure I completely understand."

He nodded once and began pacing along the peak of the roof, his hands clasped behind his back. "If you do not act you will lose her. That is the risk here. Whether or not she succeeds with this man, she will be lost."

"To the bardo?" I asked.

Banquo stopped pacing. "Best case."

I blinked. There was a worse case than the bardo? What the hell was that about?

"And if I try to reach her?"

"At its best, you will pay... you will have to take on much of her burden. At its worst, you will both be lost."

"Bardo?" Emily asked, her voice quiet and small.

"For him, yes. We might be able to pull him out. For her... I'm not sure."

I took a deep breath and looked at Emily and then back at Banquo. "I... It's... it's too much. I just met her. I..." I couldn't stand the empathy showing on their faces, so I sunk back into the house, back down to Haley and Edgar.

Edgar was now washing his dishes. Slowly, meticulously, carefully. Haley's hands were buried in his temples, the remnant of her form floating behind him in that classic ghostly look.

"I'm sorry," I said. "I can't. I... we..."

I felt a deep fatigue descend on me. I needed to rest— all ghosts need to rest. It's this dreamless nothingness called "fading." A faded ghost is just gone—where, no one really knows (and I don't think "where" is even the right way to think about it). They are gone and unreachable and don't come back until they are rested.

I could sense Emily and Banquo coming after me. I couldn't fly faster than them and they could both pop, so I gave into the fatigue and faded. Haley's words were the last thing I heard. "You will kill yourself, believe me, you will. This, right now, this will be your life until you do. I will give you no rest I will give..."

Chapter Nineteen

I was faded for about twelve hours and came to in the sweet darkness of my grave. Some ghosts, like me, rest with their bones, down in the ground where our remains are. I know it sounds weird, but there I feel calm and connected.

As I rose out of the ground, I lingered, looking at my gravestone. "Walter George Anchor, 1971–2011." That's all it said. No "Beloved Husband," I was divorced. No "Devoted Father," I had never had children. No "Cherished Son," my parents were gone when I died. Just my name and a couple of years.

"It's okay, you know," Emily said.

Her little voice shocked me.

"I don't blame you for not trying. Even Banquo doesn't. Some things are just too much." She was still wearing her shorts and her T-shirt with a lollipop on it. Today the lollipop was blue. She had very good control of her ghostly form and could change it easily. A blue lollipop generally meant that she was sad. And judging from what she was telling me, she was sad for Haley, sad for me.

"Thanks," I said.

"What now?" Emily asked. "Maybe we should go do something fun today. That house over by Fairview Avenue, they've probably got *Law and Order* on."

When Emily had been tutoring me in ghostly matters and my resolve to find my killer became clear, we had fallen into the habit of watching legal or detective shows. I wouldn't call it good training, but it was something to do.

I shook my head. "Nope. Off to the SECI chambers. Time to get in line. Time to tell this story so…" I faltered, unable to articulate what I wanted to say. Something about justice being served. Something about a wrong being righted. But it didn't feel like justice would be served for Haley or Roger or any of this man's victims. But it would prevent him taking more lives. And that was something.

Emily took my hand and smiled up at me. Her hand was so small, her face so young. We've spent a lot of time together now, but it is still disconcerting. The world jolted suddenly and then with a "pop" we stood in front of a nondescript industrial building in front of a door that said, "Afterlife Communications, Inc."

JJ LYNCH IS something of a legend around the grave-yard. Banquo tutored him and a Mexican guy named Jesus after they died. JJ dove into his afterlife and did the unthinkable. He reached his loved ones, stopped his best friend from killing himself, and killed a man in the process. He documented all of this in a memoir that he wrote in the SECI chamber.

I've never met JJ. He's been in the bardo for months,

having gone in intentionally to try to rescue someone else. He's a legend, all right, and something of a cautionary tale. Emily tells me that Banquo is shorter than usual because he worries about JJ.

So, JJ did all this writing, the people behind the SECI chamber published his memoir as a book called *Shuffled Off* (there is lots of Shakespeare at the Midnight Circle in case you recognize that phrase from Hamlet). Some of the living read the book before they died. Some of them find the SECI chambers.

That's not what this story is about, but I mention it because the wait for a SECI chamber was about five days. Lots of ghosts were in line waiting for their chance. And that gave me five days to think about what had happened since I died. To think about Haley and what she was attempting to do to her murderer. To think about my life and my afterlife.

The SECI chambers, there are three now, sit in a bland industrial space with a cement floor and a high ceiling. The ghosts waiting spiral out from those three structures. The chambers are about four feet on a side and about seven feet tall, made out of some fancy new electromagnetic (EM) shielding. They have sensors inside that detect ghostly EM emissions in very specific patterns and turn them into letters. It's complicated and I know JJ explained it thoroughly in *Shuffled Off*, so suffice it to say that it allows ghosts to type.

As we waited, Emily was great and supportive, doing her best to distract me. Teaching me how to play jacks—which is anything but easy. The jacks and the ball have to be an extension of your ghostly form, so it was quite the advanced lesson.

We got to know the other ghosts in line with us, and in general it was a pretty good time, but the closer we got to the SECI chambers, the more agitated I got. I kept thinking about Haley. What would happen to her? What fate could be worse than the bardo? Could I actually help?

There were only two ghosts in line in front of us when it became too much. "Emily…" I began.

"What is it, Walter?"

"I… Haley… I have to…"

Emily gave me the gentlest smile and grabbed my hand. "Is it time to go to her?" she asked.

My jaw dropped. Sometimes I think Emily is the wisest person I have ever known. At those moments, the wisdom of the four-year-old she was when she died and her eighty years dead come together. She is wise like a child and wise like an old person at the same time. How could she have the patience to give me this much time? How could she know to seize the moment when I gave her the smallest of openings?

"Yes," I said. "Please."

With a "pop" we were with Haley. It was not what I expected.

Chapter Twenty

"YOU ARE AS GOOD AS DEAD NOW, SO WHY NOT FINISH it? You know you don't want to live anymore. You know you are worthless. No one loves you and no one will ever love you..."

Haley's diatribe was intact but everything else had changed.

I would not have recognized her except for her voice. Haley didn't look like Haley and barely looked like a person. Her face had elongated and gone was any detail but the vaguest notion of eyes, mouth, and hair. Her form was dark grey like some great storm cloud. What passed for her arms were still attached to Edgar's head.

Edgar's transformation wasn't as dramatic, but it was significant. He sat slumped in a wheelchair, his eyes vacant, his skin pale, his jaw slack.

I looked around. We were in a plain institutional-looking room with quite a few other people. Some sat still and quiet. Others rocked and mumbled. Others looked pretty normal and sat around playing checkers or cards.

"Oh, shit," I said.

"We're in a loony bin," Emily said.

"This is bad."

"Should I go get Banquo?" Emily asked.

I shook my head. "He said I knew what to do. I don't think that has changed."

"But…" Emily began. "But this is worse, much worse than before."

I looked down at her. The worried look on her face almost stopped me. I squatted down to her level. "I have to do this, you know." She nodded. "If I don't, I won't be able to live with myself."

"But…"

"If this goes wrong, then go get Banquo." I stood up and went to Haley. She was stretched out horizontally behind Edgar's head. I carefully positioned myself in the circle of her arms. I was facing her strange-looking face and away from Edgar.

"Come back to me, Haley," I said. I then matched my form to hers—which was not easy and felt dangerous—and kissed her.

Chapter Twenty-One

IT BEGAN WITH INTENT. TO HELP HER, TO BRING HER into balance, to demonstrate my caring for her. That intent translated into action. Haley was doing what she was doing because of the feelings in her, because of the pain in her, because she had to. Those emotions flowed from her into me. I took in her anger and her pain. I took in her fear and her doubt. I took it all in.

Maybe you've experienced something like this. You spend time with a good friend who is sad or upset. You talk to them, you try to help them, and when you leave, they are better off than when you started, but you are worse. It's as if you took some of their burden from them. This was like that, but without the intervening flesh, much more rapid, much more intense, and ironically, much more real.

It just poured into me until I didn't think I could take it anymore and then it just kept coming and coming and coming.

I felt like destroying something, killing someone, making the world as miserable as I was at that moment. I needed to let some of this go, let some of it out. I wasn't aware of Haley anymore and only vaguely aware of the room, but I was aware of Edgar. He was this dark void sucking all the light out of the world. He was cruel and evil and deserved to die. He was all that was wrong with the world. I would be doing everyone a favor by ending him. It was what I could do to help.

But a patter of words, as Haley had done, was not good enough. I reached my hands—they looked like smoke —into his mind. I wasn't going to talk to him. I was going to destroy him. I could do it. If I poured all the rage I felt into his mind, it would break even further. His mind would cease to operate. He would die.

I poured all that rage and hate into him and soon I heard a sickening snap, like a bone breaking. I knew it was a piece of his mind crumbling under my attack, taking him one step closer to death.

"Walter!" I heard the voice as if from a great distance. It was a child's voice, high and light. The child was scared, terrified. Time had passed, but I had no idea how much. "Walter," she said, choking the word out amidst a storm of tears. "Please, Walter. Don't do it. I need you, Walter, I need you."

I paused and pulled my hands out of Edgar's head. She needed me? Someone needed me? I saw Emily. She looked so vulnerable in her shorts and her lollipop T-shirt. "Emily?" I said, her name coming to me. I had become something else, I wasn't Walter, I was something much more primal, but Emily, I knew Emily.

"Please, Walter, come with me." She extended her hand towards me. I didn't take it. I knew that somehow that would be bad for her. I didn't want to hurt her. She slowly moved back and I followed. She needed me, someone needed me.

It seemed impossible to leave. I wanted to return to my

revenge, but I could not deny this little girl. I could not turn my back on her.

I was vaguely aware as we flew over Tucson, the full moon illuming the city below. We came to a grassy area surrounded by trees, filled with the glow of spirits and stones of smooth granite.

"Here, Walter. Here is your place. Here are your bones. You need to rest, Walter. You'll feel better after you rest."

"I don't want to rest, I want to—"

"Please!" Emily shouted, tears running down her cheeks. "Please, Walter, you must rest. Sink into the ground, find your bones. You are tired. So tired, I know you are."

"But he deserves to die. He must..." My mind was starting to come back to me. "Haley... where is Haley?"

"She is with Banquo. You saved her. You did good, Walter. But now you must rest, you must find your bones."

I blinked and looked around. I was in the graveyard. Emily was there and many other ghosts had circled us, kind of like it was the Midnight Circle. "You saved her," Jim the cowboy said. "Rest now," his companion Jane added. "You deserve it," another ghost said with a broad smile. Many more of them spoke to me saying kind things.

I looked down at the granite stone. "Walter Anchor 1960–2011." It was a plain gravestone, but I could feel its weight. Like it was my anchor point. My bones were down there. I loved to rest with my bones. It felt so calming, so much like home.

"Justice, Emily," I said. "Justice must be served."

"It has been," Emily said quietly, the tears still running down her cheeks. "He will never hurt anyone again. You made sure of that."

"Okay," I said, feeling slightly more like myself. "I *am* tired."

"Just sink into the ground. Rest. I'll be here waiting for you. I'll always be here for you, Walter."

As I slowly sunk into the ground, I smiled. I knew Emily was there for me, she had been ever since she found me. I wasn't alone anymore. I wasn't alone.

As the earth surrounded me, I felt myself slowly calm and then I knew nothing.

Chapter Twenty-Two

EDGAR HALIFAX IS STILL ALIVE, BUT THERE IS NOT MUCH of his mind left and he won't hurt anyone ever again. First Haley, and then I, saw to that. I can't say I feel that bad about it—he was a psychotic murderer and he had it coming. What I do feel bad about is the price we had to pay. Doing something like that changes you. Doing that changed the "us" that was forming between Haley and me.

"I have to go," Haley said, her face tight, her arms crossed. Her form was back to normal, she was no longer an avenging spirit, but the cost of what had happened was clear in her haunted blue eyes. They looked much paler than I remembered.

The sun was setting over our graveyard, the thin layers of clouds and Tucson pollution putting on a good show to the west.

"Where?" I asked. I had been faded for a long time—I think about a week had passed.

"Utah," she said, her head bobbing to the north. "There is a small graveyard there in a ghost town called Silver Reef. Not too many ghosts and they've all been dead for a long time, they're all stable." She shrugged, her shoulders seeming very thin. "Banquo seems to think it will be good for me."

I nodded, but didn't know what else to say. I didn't want her to go, but after what had happened, I didn't really want her to stay either.

"I've been waiting for you to come back so I could say good-bye. I... You..."

I smiled at her. "You're welcome, Haley. I am glad I could help you. I hope things go well for you."

She leaned in and carefully kissed me on the cheek. She did it right so I could feel just the barest brush of her lips, like a feather or a rose petal. Banquo walked over and gave me a nod and took Haley by the arm. They walked a few yards away and with a "pop" were gone.

In truth, I will miss her.

"I've been thinking," Emily said. She had found me standing alone in the graveyard after Haley and Banquo had left. "I think it's time for you to upgrade your outfit."

"What?" I asked, looking down at my blue scrubs.

"You're not a dentist anymore, Walter. You are a detective. You solved Haley's murder and brought a terrible man to justice."

I shrugged. It didn't feel much like a victory. We found out about these strange happenings in my old dental office but didn't get anywhere with my own murder. I suspected there was more to learn from Wheeler, but couldn't imagine surveilling him again. We had no leads. I looked at Emily, her lollipop was a pale yellow. She was worried.

"We didn't find out who was behind the corporate espionage," I said.

She snorted and crossed her arms in front of her chest. "Let the cops chase that down once you write the story. White-collar crime is for wimps. We solve murders."

I nodded and smiled. "It was a team effort, Emily. It wouldn't have happened without you."

She put up her hand and we did a high five, our ghostly hands slapping together, a big smile on her face. The smile melted into something coy and she said, "Really? Because... well... I've heard rumor of a murder at the University that happened just last night. Maybe..."

I laughed. "You want to go investigate?"

She nodded vigorously, her blonde curls bobbing around her face. "But first you need to look the part. I'm thinking a long brown trench coat and fedora. Like Humphrey Bogart in *Casablanca*." I must have looked dubious, because she added a high-pitched "please."

I could not deny her enthusiasm, or really anything she wants, after what she has done for me. We spent the next hour working on my new form. It wasn't great—a bit vaguely shaped—but it would do, and I knew I would get better at holding it as time went by.

"There he is," she said once I was done. "Walter Anchor, ghost detective! Let's go."

I kneeled down and stared into her youthful face that hid her many years of experience. "Can I say one thing before we go?" She nodded, her eyes getting wide. "Thank you for stopping me... for what you did for me." She nodded again, her brow furrowed. "I can't do this without you." I wasn't referring to being a detective, but to "being" in general. I saw her blinking back tears, so I think she got it.

"Emily, can you give me a few minutes? I've got something I've got to do."

She looked me up and down, nodded gravely, and let go of my hand.

"This won't take long," I said, giving her my best, most reassuring smile.

THE GHOST HAD AN UNSAVORY LOOK, with small eyes and crooked teeth, dressed all in black. He leaned, in a display of faux nonchalance, against the grey stone of the crypt. I had been doing some independent investigation, there were some loose ends in regards to what had happened to Haley.

He gave me a derisive snort as a greeting. "Nice outfit," he said, the sarcasm way overdone.

"You called Galt?" I asked.

He nodded.

"You the one that taught Haley how to mess with the living?"

He nodded again. I heard some moans and the sound of metal scraping against stone. Emily had always told me to stay away from the crypts, but this was important.

"Then you and I have a problem," I said.

He shrugged and pushed himself away from the stone wall. This was all artifice. He was a ghost, the wall could not support him, and he couldn't push himself away from it. It looked real, it was well done, which led me to believe he was a mature ghost. "The girl asked nice," he said with a thin grin and a shrug. "How could I turn her down?"

I crossed my arms and shook my head. "You should have turned her down. What happened is on you."

He chuckled, it was dry and thin and sounded dangerous. "The girl had a choice. She chose to come to me. She chose to do what she did."

"That may be, but if I ever see you so much as speaking to Emily, or any of my other friends, I will destroy you."

He slowly smiled, showing his crooked teeth off. "First off, that old witch Emily can take care of herself. Secondly, I see why you and Haley got along so well."

"What?"

"What she did to her killer, is that how you would 'destroy' me? You're just like Haley—you'll do what it takes to settle a score."

"I... No, that's not what I meant."

He held his hands up. "Relax, I appreciate the sentiment. You are willing to defend what is yours. I understand that. Maybe you and I aren't so different. Maybe you and I could be friends. Maybe I could show you a few things Emily and Banquo won't show you."

His words rattled around my head. What did he know? Would I act differently than Haley if I found my killer?

"Look," I finally said, "just stay away from Emily. Got it?"

He smiled and slumped back against the crypt wall. "Yeah, I got it. No problem. I do favors for my friends all the time."

As I walked away from him, I knew Galt and I weren't done, but Emily was waiting and there was another murder to solve.

More Mystery?

WALTER AND EMILY HAVE A LOT MORE CASES TO SOLVE. Next is "The Ghost Bride's Gift," available now. Join my email newsletter and never miss a thing.

The Ghost Bride's Gift

Walter Anchor wants to solve his own murder, but with no leads and nothing else to do he solves other murders to pass the time.

When his best ghost-friend Emily finds a dead bride alone in a hotel without a scratch on her, things go from bad to worse for Walter. The bride looks just like his ex-wife. Seeing her forces Walter to come face-to-face with a past he wants to forget.

Can Walter reconcile with his past in time to solve the

murder and save the ghost bride from the ghostly hell known as the bardo?

From the author of *Shuffled Off: A Ghost's Memoir* comes a mystery unlike anything seen before.

Get "The Ghost Brides's Gift" Now!

About the Author

Robert J. McCarter is the author of seven novels, three novellas, and dozens of short stories. He is a finalist for the *Writers of the Future* contest and his stories have appeared or are forthcoming in *The Saturday Evening Post*, *Pulphouse Fiction Magazine*, *Fiction River*, *Andromeda Spaceways Inflight Magazine*, and numerous anthologies.

His latest effort is a serialized novel called *Woody and June Versus the Apocalypse*, a story of adventure and love and taking things (even the apocalypse) in stride. Of his novel, *Seeing Forever*, Kirkus Reviews says, "Sci-fi as it should be: engaging, moving, and grand in scope."

He lives in the mountains of Arizona with his amazing wife and his ridiculously adorable dogs.

Find out more at:
robertjmccarter.com

Books by Robert J. McCarter

Walter Anchor, Ghost Detective Stories

- **Case 1: Detecting Haley** (also part of *Life After: Stories of Life, Death, and the Places in Between*)
- **Case 2: The Ghost Bride's Gift**
- **Case 3: A Long Hard Fall** (coming March, 2020)
- **Case 4: Death of a Dentist** (coming May, 2020)
- **Case 5: A Hollywood Kind of a Murder** (coming July 2020)
- **Case 6: The Red Arrow Murders** (coming September, 2020)
- **Unfinished Business: The Cases of Walter Anchor Ghost Detective** (coming October, 2020)

For a complete list of Walter Anchor stories, go to RobertJMcCarter.com/WalterAnchor

Novels in the "Ghost's Memoir" world:

- Shuffled Off: A Ghost's Memoir, Book 1
- Drawing the Dead
- To Be a Fool: A Ghost's Memoir, Book 2
- Of Things Not Seen: A Ghost's Memoir, Book 3
- A Boy, a Girl, and a Ghost

For a complete list the "Ghost's Memoir" novels, go to ShuffledOff.com

The Wood and June versus the Apocalypse series

Find out more at WoodyAndJune.com

The Neutrinoman and Lightningirl Series

Find out more at Neutrinoman.com

Other Novels:

- Seeing Forever

For a more information, go to RobertJMcCarter.com